APPEARANCE AND REALITY

NAVEEN SHARMA

Contents

Foreword   *v*

Appearance And Reality

Faith And Doubt   9

Foreword

Dear readers,

"A book is like a selfless friend that seeks only to share with you whatever it has, without expecting anything in return. Therefore it is necessary for every reader to give some respect to the books. There is a big difference between a reader and a good reader. A reader just tries to read but a good reader not only reads but also tries to make an interaction between himself and the writer for understanding the content of the book in a better way. A good reader keeps patience and avoids to be in hurry while reading. Therefore, try to be a good reader instead of being a particular reader."

Appearance and Reality

This story starts with the arrival of Michael Faustus in the city of London, who is a famous businessman in New York. He comes London for business purpose. After some days of his arrival, he comes to know that his friend Stuart Rochester, a famous industrialist of London, also lives here with his wife Elizabeth Rochester. After knowing about Stuart and his wife's presence in London, Michael invites both of them to his home for spending time. Then, after getting invitation from Michael, they go to his home, next day. Michael greets them and proves himself to be a good host. But, the beauty of Elizabeth's face attracts him and he finds himself fall in love with her. Both guests do not have any intension about this mentality of their host. They spend approximate four days in his home with so much happiness, and on fifth day, they decide to return back but before returning, they invite Michael to their home. He feels happy to get the invitation because he himself wanted to get the invitation from them for spending some more time with Elizabeth. His affection for her has reached on its peak, so, now he does not want to miss any chance to be in contact with her.

And, one day, he goes to Rochester house for spending some time with Elizabeth. When he reaches there, he comes to know that only she is at home because Mr. Rochester has gone somewhere for some hours. Michael starts facing a conflict in his mind "I should tell her about my feelings or not". After a long inner conflict, he decides to tell each and everything whatever he thinks about her.

At that time, Elizabeth prepares food for her guest, she feels happy to host him because she is a very friendly natured woman. After completing her work, she sits with her guest to have some conversation. He feels that she is in very good mood, so, he finds it the best chance to tell her about his affection. Then, without wasting time, he asks her to say something.

She says "Yes, you can say whatever you want to say". Then he starts revealing things in very emotional manner. He tries his best to convince her but he gets failure. She replies that she respects his feelings but she is married. But, he does not want to accept her excuses. He says that he will try his best to make her feel happy, if she accepts his love. After listening his words she refuses again and replies in a calm manner, sorry, but i love my husband very much. She says, it is not a good thing for a married woman to start life with a strange man.

Therefore; she requests him to talk on any other topic because that topic is totally baseless. At the same time, he says, sorry for wasting her precious time and returns back to his home.

Now, Michael feels disappointment for being refused by Elizabeth, but when he realizes, he finds her reply to be logical. He thinks her marriage to be the biggest obstacle in front of him. Therefore, he makes plan in his mind to disturb married life of both of them, so that, he can have a chance to complete his desire. For completing his motive, he appoints a man in exchange of ten thousand ponds.

The person whom he appoints is his friend, Tom William. He starts making plan to convince Stuart that his wife is cheating with him and is having an affair with a man, named, Tom William.

First of all, he meets Stuart to have a conversation in which he talks to him in a normal way but in last he narrates him a story in which a wife cheats her husband and makes relationship with a strange man even after being married.

After listening this story, Stuart feels happy because he thinks that his wife is very faithful towards him and totally opposite from the wife of Michael's story. But, Michael thinks that he has put seed of doubt in Stuart's mind. During this incident, Michael sees a very beautiful handkerchief in Stuart's hand. He praises the beauty of that handkerchief. Then Stuart replies that it was given to him by his wife Elizabeth. Now, another plan takes birth in his clever mind in which he decides to use handkerchief as a tool.

He goes back to home and tells his plan to Tom William. He makes him understand about his role in this plan.

Tom promises him to do whatever Michael has said.

Michael purchases exactly that kind of handkerchief which he had seen in Stuart's hand. After that, according to plan, Michael invites Stuart to his home and starts preparing things according to plan. After some time, Stuart arrives and starts talking with Michael. At the same time, Tom comes outside from his room and appears in front of them. Then, Michael asks Stuart about him. Stuart introduces him and says, now he also lives with him in the same house because of having a strong bond of friendship between them.

At the same time, Tom offers them to come in his room. At that moment, they all go to his room and talk to each other, just then, Tom tries to show his handkerchief to Stuart, according to plan. After seeing it, he says "It is exactly like my handkerchief, wow." Then, Tom says "This was given to me by my lover." Stuart shows intension to listen about his lover, then, Tom says that his lover's name is Elizabeth and they both love each other very much. Stuarts asks, Is she married? Tom answers "Yes, but she is not happy with her husband."

Now, Stuart shows him the picture of his wife and asks, Is she your lover?

Tom says "Yes but how do you know her?" Stuart does not answer but says "Don't worry, she is only your lover, nothing else."

After some time, Stuart remembers the story which was narrated to him by Michael and compares it with his real life. He asks Michael that did you know about it already? He says, yes, that's why I told you that story for giving you a hint about your wife's unfaithfulness. After listening these words he starts going to his home.

Now, as expected by Michael, Stuart starts behaving with Elizabeth in a rude manner, now, he does not give her that respect which he used to give her. She bears his change in behavior but does not react much. She is not happy with him now. Stuarts thinks that he should continue his rude behavior as a revenge against her betray towards him.

After some days, Michael meets Elizabeth when Stuart is not present at home. He talks to her in a simple way and asks to her about her married life with her husband. She becomes emotional and starts weeping. Then, she tells him about the rude behavior of Stuart towards her. She says that she is not happy with him now. Michael gets satisfied because everything was happening according to his plan. Meanwhile, he says "If you are not happy with him then you should leave him and start a new life, you should not bear his rudeness anymore." She takes his words seriously and tries to do things according to his suggestion.

On the other hand, Tom William falls in love with a beautiful girl, named Jane. He decides to propose her and executes it as well.

Jane says that if he really loves her then he should be loyal towards him and should tell everything about himself, only truth.

Tom does not want to lose her, so he tells all the things and tells about his services towards Michael for disturbing married life of Stuart and Elizabeth. She says that she will accept his love, if he stops giving his services to Michael. Tom, without any doubt, accepts her order because he really loves her.

At Rochester house, Stuarts behaves rudely with Elizabeth as usual, but this time; she does not bear it and says, if you do not want to talk to her in a good manner then you should leave me and give divorce. He thinks in his mind that she wants to live Tom that's why she is demanding for divorce, so, he promises her to leave her soon.

At the same time, Jane comes to their home and tells them about the planning of Michael for disturbing their married life so that he could complete his desire of living with Elizabeth. She tells them each and everything and tells that how they were used by him like toys. She requests to forgive Tom because real culprit is Michael.

After listening truth they both blame themselves to let themselves be used by Michael and for losing trust of each other. They both say sorry to each other for their mistakes, promise to trust on each other all the time.

Now Jane says "It is not compulsory that whatever is appearing, it will be true always, sometimes appearance and reality are totally opposite from each, as happened in this case."

She says "Stuart should have talked to his wife before accepting talks of Michael about her."

Now, she requests both of them to not lose their trust and respect for each other because these are the two most important things for maintaining a healthy relationship. If there is faith then there is no place for doubt but if doubt comes in existence then faith cannot exist.

After listening this precious moral of Jane, both husband and wife accept their mistakes. They say from Jane that they have learnt from mistakes and will not repeat them regain for living their remaining life with peace and harmony.

Now, Michael comes to know about the news of reunion of Stuart and Elizabeth by someone. Then, he kills himself by drinking poison for getting failed in his task to win Elizabeth.

After some days, Tom and Jane get married to each other. Jane demands promise from Tom that he will lose his trust on her. Tom promises her for this and says to try his best for being a good husband. Jane also says the same thing.

In the last, Tom, Jane, Stuart and Elizabeth visit the grave of Michael Faustus and pray from God for the salvation of his soul. Then both married couples return back to their destinations and live their married life with happiness.

Faith And Doubt

When we trust on someone, when we have positive beliefs and positive thoughts for someone or something, and we do not have any kind of doubt to accept someone or something, then we can say it's a kind of faith. Sometimes, faith is considered as the synonym of strong religious belief because faith is the primary stage to accept any religion.

On the other hand, when we are not willing to accept something or somebody. Most of the times, it is considered as the feeling of uncertainty.

www.ingramcontent.com/pod-product-compliance
Lightning Source LLC
Chambersburg PA
CBHW022047150726
47990CB00004B/1642